Adventures of Frog and Toad

By Arnold Lobel

FROG AND TOAD ARE FRIENDS

FROG AND TOAD TOGETHER

DAYS WITH FROG AND TOAD

BARNES
&NOBLE
B O O K S
N E W   Y O R K

Frog and Toad Are Friends

For Barbara Borack

HarperCollins®, ☰®, Harper Trophy®, and I Can Read Book®
are trademarks of HarperCollins Publishers Inc.

HarperCollins®, ☰®, Harper Trophy®, and I Can Read Book®
are trademarks of HarperCollins Publishers Inc.
Frog and Toad Are Friends
Copyright © 1970 by Arnold Lobel

Library of Congress Catalog Card Number: 73-105492
ISBN 0-06-444020-6 (pbk.)
First published in 1970.
First Harper Trophy edition, 1979.

Contents

Spring

Frog ran up the path
to Toad's house.

He knocked on the front door.

There was no answer.

"Toad, Toad," shouted Frog,

"wake up. It is spring!"

"Blah," said a voice
from inside the house.

"Toad! Toad!" cried Frog.

4

"The sun is shining!

The snow is melting. Wake up!"

"I am not here," said the voice.

Frog walked into the house.

It was dark.

All the shutters were closed.

"Toad, where are you?" called Frog.

"Go away," said the voice

from a corner of the room.

Toad was lying in bed.

6

He had pulled all the covers
over his head.

Frog pushed Toad out of bed.

He pushed him out of the house
and onto the front porch.

Toad blinked in the bright sun.

"Help!" said Toad.

"I cannot see anything."

"Don't be silly," said Frog.

"What you see

is the clear warm light of April.

And it means

that we can begin

a whole new year together, Toad.

Think of it," said Frog.

"We will skip through the meadows

and run through the woods

and swim in the river.

In the evenings we will sit

right here on this front porch

and count the stars."

"You can count them, Frog,"
said Toad. "I will be too tired.
I am going back to bed."

Toad went back into the house.

He got into the bed

and pulled the covers

over his head again.

"But, Toad," cried Frog,

"you will miss all the fun!"

"Listen, Frog," said Toad.

"How long have I been asleep?"

"You have been asleep
since November," said Frog.
"Well then," said Toad,
"a little more sleep
will not hurt me.
Come back again and wake me up
at about half past May.
Good night, Frog."

"But, Toad," said Frog,

"I will be lonely until then."

Toad did not answer.

He had fallen asleep.

Frog looked at Toad's calendar.

The November page was still on top.

Frog tore off the November page.

He tore off the December page.

And the January page,

the February page,

and the March page.

He came to the April page.

Frog tore off the April page too.

Then Frog ran back to Toad's bed.

"Toad, Toad, wake up. It is May now."

"What?" said Toad.

"Can it be May so soon?"

"Yes," said Frog.

"Look at your calendar."

Toad looked at the calendar.

The May page was on top.

"Why, it *is* May!" said Toad
as he climbed out of bed.
Then he and Frog
ran outside
to see how the world
was looking in the spring.

The Story

One day in summer
Frog was not feeling well.
Toad said, "Frog,
you are looking quite green."
"But I always look green,"
said Frog. "I am a frog."
"Today you look very green
even for a frog," said Toad.
"Get into my bed and rest."

Toad made Frog a cup of hot tea.

Frog drank the tea, and then he said,

"Tell me a story while I am resting."

"All right," said Toad.

"Let me think of a story to tell you."

Toad thought and thought.

But he could not think of a story
to tell Frog.

18

"I will go out on the front porch
and walk up and down," said Toad.
"Perhaps that will help me
to think of a story."
Toad walked up and down
on the porch for a long time.
But he could not think of a story
to tell Frog.

Then Toad went into the house

and stood on his head.

"Why are you standing

on your head?" asked Frog.

"I hope that if I stand on my head,

it will help me

to think of a story," said Toad.

Toad stood on his head
for a long time.
But he could not think
of a story to tell Frog.

21

Then Toad poured a glass of water
over his head.

"Why are you pouring water
over your head?" asked Frog.

"I hope that if I pour water
over my head,
it will help me to think
of a story," said Toad.

Toad poured many glasses of water
over his head.

But he could not think
of a story to tell Frog.

Then Toad began
to bang his head
against the wall.

"Why are you banging your head
against the wall?" asked Frog.
"I hope that if I bang my head
against the wall hard enough,
it will help me to think of a story,"
said Toad.

"I am feeling much better now, Toad,"
said Frog. "I do not think
I need a story anymore."
"Then you get out of bed
and let me get into it," said Toad,
"because now I feel terrible."
Frog said, "Would you like me
to tell you a story, Toad?"
"Yes," said Toad, "if you know one."

"Once upon a time," said Frog,
"there were two good friends,
a frog and a toad.

The frog was not feeling well.

He asked his friend the toad

to tell him a story.

The toad could not think of a story.

He walked up and down on the porch,

but he could not think of a story.

He stood on his head,

but he could not think of a story.

He poured water over his head,

but he could not think of a story.

26

He banged his head against the wall,

but he still could not think

of a story.

Then the toad did not feel so well,

and the frog was feeling better.

So the toad went to bed

and the frog got up

and told him a story.

The end.

How was that,

Toad?" said Frog.

But Toad did not answer.

He had fallen asleep.

27

A Lost Button

Toad and Frog

went for a long walk.

They walked across

a large meadow.

They walked in the woods.

They walked along the river.

At last they went back home

to Toad's house.

"Oh, drat," said Toad.

"Not only do my feet hurt,
but I have lost
one of the buttons on my jacket."

"Don't worry," said Frog.

"We will go back

to all the places where we walked.

We will soon find your button."

They walked back to the large meadow.

They began to look for the button

in the tall grass.

"Here is your button!" cried Frog.

"That is not my button," said Toad.

"That button is black.

My button was white."

Toad put the black button

in his pocket.

A sparrow flew down.

"Excuse me," said the sparrow.

"Did you lose a button? I found one."

"That is not my button," said Toad.

"That button has two holes.

My button had four holes."

Toad put the button with two holes

in his pocket.

They went back to the woods

and looked on the dark paths.

"Here is your button," said Frog.

"That is not my button," cried Toad.

"That button is small.

My button was big."

Toad put the small button

in his pocket.

A raccoon came out from behind a tree.

"I heard that you were looking

for a button," he said.

"Here is one that I just found."

"That is not my button!" wailed Toad.

"That button is square.

My button was round."

Toad put the square button

in his pocket.

Frog and Toad went back to the river.

They looked for the button
in the mud.

"Here is your button," said Frog.

"That is not my button!" shouted Toad.

"That button is thin.

My button was thick."

Toad put the thin button
in his pocket. He was very angry.
He jumped up and down
and screamed,
"The whole world
is covered with buttons,
and not one of them is mine!"

Toad ran home and slammed the door.

There, on the floor,

he saw his white, four-holed,

big, round, thick button.

"Oh," said Toad.

"It was here all the time.

What a lot of trouble

I have made for Frog."

Toad took all of the buttons
out of his pocket.

He took his sewing box
down from the shelf.

Toad sewed the buttons
all over his jacket.

The next day Toad gave

his jacket to Frog.

Frog thought that it was beautiful.

He put it on and jumped for joy.

None of the buttons fell off.

Toad had sewed them on very well.

A Swim

Toad and Frog
went down to the river.
"What a day for a swim," said Frog.
"Yes," said Toad.
"I will go behind these rocks
and put on my bathing suit."
"I don't wear a bathing suit,"
said Frog.
"Well, I do," said Toad.

"After I put on my bathing suit,
you must not look at me
until I get into the water."

"Why not?"

asked Frog.

"Because I look funny

in my bathing suit.

That is why," said Toad.

Frog closed his eyes when Toad

came out from behind the rocks.

Toad was wearing his bathing suit.

"Don't peek," he said.

Frog and Toad jumped

into the water.

They swam all afternoon.

Frog swam fast

and made big splashes.

Toad swam slowly

and made smaller splashes.

A turtle came along the riverbank.

"Frog, tell that turtle

to go away," said Toad.

"I do not want him to see me

in my bathing suit

when I come out of the river."

Frog swam over to the turtle.

"Turtle," said Frog,

"you will have to go away."

"Why should I?" asked the turtle.

"Because Toad thinks that

he looks funny in his bathing suit,

and he does not want you to see him,"

said Frog.

Some lizards were sitting nearby.

"Does Toad really look funny

in his bathing suit?" they asked.

A snake crawled out of the grass.

"If Toad looks funny

in his bathing suit," said the snake,

"then I, for one, want to see him."

"We want to see him too,"
said two dragonflies.

"Me too," said a field mouse.
"I have not seen anything funny
in a long time."

Frog swam back to Toad.

"I am sorry, Toad," he said. "Everyone wants to see how you will look."

"Then I will stay right here until they go away," said Toad.

The turtle and the lizards and the snake and the dragonflies and the field mouse all sat on the riverbank.

They waited for Toad to come out of the water.

"Please," cried Frog, "please go away!"

But no one went away.

Toad was getting colder and colder.

He was beginning to shiver and sneeze.

"I will have to come out of the water,"

said Toad. "I am catching a cold."

Toad climbed

out of the river.

The water dripped

out of his bathing suit

and down onto his feet.

The turtle laughed.

The lizards laughed.

The snake laughed.

The field mouse laughed,

and Frog laughed.

"What are you laughing at, Frog?"
said Toad.

"I am laughing at you, Toad,"
said Frog,

"because you *do* look funny
in your bathing suit."

"Of course I do," said Toad.
Then he picked up his clothes
and went home.

The Letter

Toad was sitting on his front porch.

Frog came along and said,

"What is the matter, Toad?

You are looking sad."

"Yes," said Toad.

"This is my sad time of day.

It is the time

when I wait for the mail to come.

It always makes me very unhappy."

"Why is that?" asked Frog.

"Because I never get any mail,"

said Toad.

"Not ever?" asked Frog.

"No, never," said Toad.

"No one has ever sent me a letter.

Every day my mailbox is empty.

That is why waiting for the mail

is a sad time for me."

Frog and Toad sat on the porch,

feeling sad together.

Then Frog said,

"I have to go home now, Toad.

There is something that I must do."

Frog hurried home.

He found a pencil

and a piece of paper.

He wrote on the paper.

He put the paper in an envelope.

On the envelope he wrote

"A LETTER FOR TOAD."

Frog ran out of his house.

He saw a snail that he knew.

"Snail," said Frog, "please take

this letter to Toad's house

and put it in his mailbox."

"Sure," said the snail. "Right away."

Then Frog ran back to Toad's house.

Toad was in bed, taking a nap.

"Toad," said Frog,

"I think you should get up

and wait for the mail some more."

"No," said Toad,

"I am tired of waiting for the mail."

Frog looked out of the window
at Toad's mailbox.

The snail was not there yet.

"Toad," said Frog, "you never know
when someone may send you a letter."

"No, no," said Toad. "I do not think
anyone will ever send me a letter."

Frog looked out of the window.

The snail was not there yet.

"But, Toad," said Frog,

"someone may send you a letter today."

"Don't be silly," said Toad.

"No one has ever sent me

a letter before, and no one

will send me a letter today."

Frog looked out of the window.

The snail was still not there.

"Frog, why do you keep looking

out of the window?" asked Toad.

"Because now I am waiting

for the mail," said Frog.

"But there will not be any," said Toad.

"Oh, yes there will," said Frog,

"because I have sent you a letter."

"You have?" said Toad.

"What did you write in the letter?"

Frog said, "I wrote

'Dear Toad, I am glad

that you are my best friend.

Your best friend, Frog.'"

"Oh," said Toad,

"that makes a very good letter."

Then Frog and Toad went out

onto the front porch

to wait for the mail.

They sat there,

feeling happy together.

Frog and Toad waited a long time.

Four days later

the snail got to Toad's house

and gave him the letter from Frog.

Toad was very pleased to have it.

Frog and Toad Together

by Arnold Lobel

HarperTrophy®

A Division of HarperCollinsPublishers

For Barbara Dicks

Library of Congress Catalog Card Number: 72-183163
ISBN 0-06-444021-4
First Harper Trophy edition, 1979.

Contents

A List

One morning Toad sat in bed.

"I have many things to do," he said.

"I will write them

all down on a list

so that I can remember them."

Toad wrote on a piece of paper:

A List of things to do today

Then he wrote:

Wake up

4

"I have done that," said Toad,

and he crossed out:

~~Wake up~~

Then Toad wrote other things
on the paper.

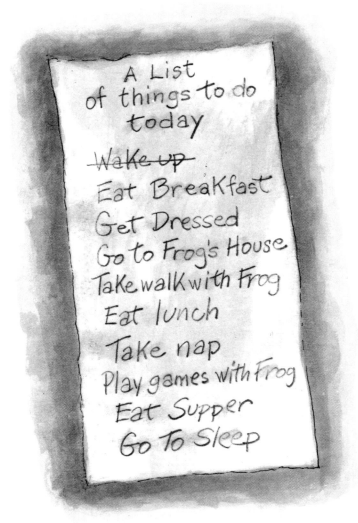

A List
of things to do
today

Wake up
Eat Breakfast
Get Dressed
Go to Frog's House
Take walk with Frog
Eat lunch
Take nap
Play games with Frog
Eat Supper
Go To Sleep

"There," said Toad.

"Now my day

is all written down."

He got out of bed

and had something to eat.

Then Toad crossed out:

~~Eat Breakfast~~

Toad took his clothes

out of the closet

and put them on.

Then he crossed out:

~~Get Dressed~~

Toad put the list in his pocket.

He opened the door

and walked out into the morning.

Soon Toad was at Frog's front door.

He took the list from his pocket

and crossed out:

~~Go to Frog's House~~

9

Toad knocked at the door.

"Hello," said Frog.

"Look at my list
of things to do,"
said Toad.

"Oh," said Frog,
"that is very nice."

Toad said, "My list tells me
that we will go
for a walk."

"All right," said Frog.
"I am ready."

Frog and Toad

went on a long walk.

Then Toad took the list

from his pocket again.

He crossed out:

~~Take walk with Frog~~

Just then there was a strong wind.

It blew the list

out of Toad's hand.

The list blew high up

into the air.

12

"Help!" cried Toad.

"My list is blowing away.

What will I do without my list?"

"Hurry!" said Frog.

"We will run and catch it."

"No!" shouted Toad.

"I cannot do that."

"Why not?" asked Frog.

"Because," wailed Toad,

"running after my list

is not one of the things

that I wrote

on my list of things to do!"

14

Frog ran after the list.

He ran over hills and swamps,

but the list blew on and on.

At last Frog came back to Toad.

"I am sorry," gasped Frog,

"but I could not catch

your list."

"Blah," said Toad.

"I cannot remember any of the things
that were on my list of things to do.
I will just have to sit here
and do nothing," said Toad.
Toad sat and did nothing.
Frog sat with him.

After a long time Frog said,
"Toad, it is getting dark.
We should be going to sleep now."

16

Go to sleep!" shouted Toad.

That was the last thing on my list!"

Toad wrote on the ground

with a stick: Go to sleep

Then he crossed out:

~~Go to sleep~~

There," said Toad.

Now my day

s all crossed out!"

I am glad,"

said Frog.

Then Frog and Toad

went right to sleep.

The Garden

Frog was in his garden.

Toad came walking by.

"What a fine garden

you have, Frog," he said.

"Yes," said Frog. "It is very nice,

but it was hard work."

"I wish I had a garden," said Toad.

"Here are some flower seeds.

Plant them in the ground," said Frog,

"and soon you will have a garden."

"How soon?" asked Toad.

"Quite soon," said Frog.

19

Toad ran home.

He planted the flower seeds.

"Now seeds," said Toad,

"start growing."

Toad walked up and down

a few times.

The seeds did not start to grow.

Toad put his head
close to the ground
and said loudly,
"Now seeds, start growing!"
Toad looked at the ground again.
The seeds did not start to grow.

Toad put his head

very close to the ground and shouted,

"NOW SEEDS, START GROWING!"

Frog came running up the path.

"What is all this noise?" he asked.

"My seeds will not grow," said Toad.

"You are shouting too much,"

said Frog. "These poor seeds

are afraid to grow."

"My seeds are afraid to grow?"

asked Toad.

"Of course," said Frog.

"Leave them alone for a few days.

Let the sun shine on them,

let the rain fall on them.

Soon your seeds will start to grow."

That night

Toad looked out of his window.

"Drat!" said Toad.

"My seeds have not

started to grow.

They must be afraid of the dark."

Toad went out to his garden

with some candles.

"I will read the seeds a story,"

said Toad.

"Then they will not be afraid."

24

Toad read a long story
to his seeds.

All the next day
Toad sang songs
to his seeds.

And all the next day
Toad read poems
to his seeds.

And all the next day
Toad played music
for his seeds.

Toad looked at the ground.

The seeds still did not

start to grow.

"What shall I do?" cried Toad.

"These must be

the most frightened seeds

in the whole world!"

Then Toad felt very tired,

and he fell asleep.

"Toad, Toad, wake up," said Frog.

"Look at your garden!"

Toad looked at his garden.

Little green plants were coming up

out of the ground.

28

"At last," shouted Toad,
"my seeds have stopped
being afraid to grow!"
"And now you will have
a nice garden too," said Frog.
"Yes," said Toad,
"but you were right, Frog.
It was very hard work."

Cookies

Toad baked some cookies.

"These cookies smell very good,"
said Toad.

He ate one.

"And they taste even better," he said

Toad ran to Frog's house.

"Frog, Frog," cried Toad,

"taste these cookies

that I have made."

30

Frog ate one of the cookies.

"These are the best cookies

I have ever eaten!" said Frog.

Frog and Toad ate many cookies,
one after another.

"You know, Toad," said Frog,
with his mouth full,
"I think we should stop eating.
We will soon be sick."

"You are right," said Toad.

"Let us eat one last cookie,

and then we will stop."

Frog and Toad ate

one last cookie.

There were many cookies

left in the bowl.

"Frog," said Toad,

"let us eat one very last cookie,

and then we will stop."

Frog and Toad

ate one very last cookie.

"We must stop eating!" cried Toad

as he ate another.

"Yes," said Frog,

reaching for a cookie,

"we need will power."

"What is will power?" asked Toad.

34

"Will power is trying hard

not to do something

that you really want to do,"

said Frog.

"You mean like trying *not*

to eat all of these cookies?"

asked Toad.

"Right," said Frog.

Frog put the cookies in a box.

"There," he said.

"Now we will not eat

any more cookies."

"But we can open the box,"

said Toad.

"That is true," said Frog.

36

Frog tied some string
around the box.
"There," he said.
"Now we will not eat
any more cookies."
"But we can cut the string
and open the box," said Toad.
"That is true," said Frog.

Frog got a ladder.

He put the box up on a high shelf.

"There," said Frog.

"Now we will not eat

any more cookies."

"But we can climb the ladder

and take the box

down from the shelf

and cut the string

and open the box,"

said Toad.

"That is true," said Frog.

Frog climbed the ladder

and took the box

down from the shelf.

He cut the string

and opened the box.

Frog took the box outside.

He shouted in a loud voice,

"HEY BIRDS,

HERE ARE COOKIES!"

Birds came from everywhere.

They picked up all the cookies

in their beaks and flew away.

"Now we have no more cookies to eat,"

said Toad sadly.

"Not even one."

"Yes," said Frog,

"but we have lots and lots

of will power."

"You may keep it all, Frog,"

said Toad.

"I am going home now

to bake a cake."

Dragons and Giants

Frog and Toad

were reading a book together.

"The people in this book

are brave," said Toad.

"They fight dragons and giants,

and they are never afraid."

"I wonder if we are brave,"

said Frog.

Frog and Toad looked into a mirror.

"We look brave," said Frog.

"Yes, but are we?"

asked Toad.

Frog and Toad went outside.

"We can try to climb this mountain,"
said Frog. "That should tell us
if we are brave."

Frog went leaping over rocks,
and Toad came puffing up
behind him.

They came to a dark cave.

A big snake came out of the cave.

"Hello lunch," said the snake

when he saw Frog and Toad.

He opened his wide mouth.

Frog and Toad jumped away.

Toad was shaking.

"I am not afraid!" he cried.

They climbed higher,

and they heard a loud noise.

Many large stones

were rolling down the mountain.

"It's an avalanche!" cried Toad.

Frog and Toad jumped away.

Frog was trembling.

"I am not afraid!" he shouted.

They came to the top

of the mountain.

The shadow of a hawk

fell over them.

Frog and Toad

jumped under a rock.

The hawk flew away.

48

"We are not afraid!"

screamed Frog and Toad

at the same time.

Then they ran down the mountain

very fast.

They ran past the place

where they saw the avalanche.

They ran past the place

where they saw the snake.

They ran all the way

to Toad's house.

"Frog, I am glad to have
a brave friend like you," said Toad.
He jumped into the bed
and pulled the covers
over his head.
"And I am happy to know
a brave person like you, Toad,"
said Frog.
He jumped into the closet
and shut the door.
Toad stayed in the bed,
and Frog stayed in the closet.

They stayed there

for a long time,

just feeling very brave together.

The Dream

Toad was asleep,

and he was having a dream.

He was on a stage,

and he was wearing

a costume.

Toad looked out

into the dark.

Frog was sitting

in the theater.

52

A strange voice from far away said,

"PRESENTING THE GREATEST TOAD

IN ALL THE WORLD!"

Toad took a deep bow.

Frog looked smaller

as he shouted,

"Hooray for Toad!"

"TOAD WILL NOW

PLAY THE PIANO VERY WELL,"

said the strange voice.

Toad played the piano,

and he did not miss a note.

"Frog," cried Toad,

"can you play the piano like this?"

"No," said Frog.

It seemed to Toad

that Frog looked even smaller.

55

"TOAD WILL NOW WALK

ON A HIGH WIRE,

AND HE WILL NOT FALL DOWN,"

said the voice.

Toad walked on the high wire.

"Frog," cried Toad,

"can you do tricks like this?"

"No," peeped Frog,

who looked very, very small.

"TOAD WILL NOW DANCE,

AND HE WILL BE WONDERFUL,"

said the voice.

58

"Frog, can you be as wonderful

as this?" said Toad

as he danced all over the stage.

There was no answer.

Toad looked out into the theater.

Frog was so small

that he could not be seen or heard.

"Frog," said Toad,

"where are you?"

There was still no answer.

"Frog, what have I done?"

cried Toad.

Then the voice said,

"THE GREATEST TOAD WILL NOW. . ."

"Shut up!" screamed Toad.

"Frog, Frog, where have you gone?"

Toad was spinning in the dark.

"Come back, Frog," he shouted.

"I will be lonely!"

"I am right here," said Frog.

Frog was standing near Toad's bed.

"Wake up, Toad," he said.

"Frog, is that really you?" said Toad.

"Of course it is me," said Frog.

"And are you

your own right size?" asked Toad.

"Yes, I think so," said Frog.

Toad looked at the sunshine

coming through the window.

"Frog," he said,

"I am so glad

that you came over."

"I always do," said Frog.

Then Frog and Toad

ate a big breakfast.

And after that

they spent a fine, long day together.

64

Days With
Frog and Toad

by Arnold Lobel

An I CAN READ Book®

HarperTrophy®
A Division of HarperCollins*Publishers*

For Liz Gordon

A portion of this book previously appeared in *Cricket*.

Days with Frog and Toad
Copyright © 1979 by Arnold Lobel
All rights reserved. No part of this book may be
used or reproduced in any manner whatsoever without
written permission except in the case of brief quotations
embodied in critical articles and reviews. Printed in
the United States of America. For information address
HarperCollins Children's Books, a division of HarperCollins
Publishers, 10 East 53rd Street, New York, NY 10022.

Library of Congress Cataloging-in-Publication Data
Lobel, Arnold.
    Days with Frog and Toad.

    (An I can read book)
    SUMMARY: Frog and Toad spend their days together, but
find sometimes it's nice to be alone.
    [1. Frogs—Fiction.   2. Toads—Fiction.   3. Friend-
ship—Fiction]   I. Title
PZ7.L7795Day   [E]   78-21786
ISBN 0-06-023963-8
ISBN 0-06-023964-6 (lib. bdg.)
ISBN 0-06-444058-3 (pbk.)

Contents

Tomorrow

Toad woke up.

"Drat!" he said.

"This house is a mess.

I have so much work to do."

Frog looked through the window.

"Toad, you are right,"

said Frog. "It is a mess."

Toad pulled the covers

over his head.

"I will do it tomorrow,"

said Toad.

"Today I will take life easy."

Frog came into the house.

"Toad," said Frog,

"your pants and jacket

are lying on the floor."

"Tomorrow," said Toad

from under the covers.

"Your kitchen sink

is filled with dirty dishes,"

said Frog.

"Tomorrow," said Toad.

"There is dust on your chairs."

"Tomorrow," said Toad.

"Your windows need scrubbing,"
said Frog.

"Your plants need watering."

"Tomorrow!" cried Toad.

"I will do it all tomorrow!"

Toad sat on the edge
of his bed.

"Blah," said Toad.

"I feel down in the dumps."

"Why?" asked Frog.

"I am thinking
about tomorrow,"
said Toad.

"I am thinking about
all of the many things
that I will have to do."

"Yes," said Frog,
"tomorrow will be
a very hard day for you."

9

"But Frog," said Toad,
"if I pick up my pants
and jacket right now,
then I will not have to
pick them up tomorrow, will I?"
"No," said Frog.
"You will not have to."
Toad picked up his clothes.
He put them in the closet.

"Frog," said Toad,

"if I wash my dishes right now,

then I will not have to

wash them tomorrow, will I?"

"No," said Frog.

"You will not have to."

Toad washed and dried his dishes.

He put them in the cupboard.

"Frog," said Toad,

"if I dust my chairs

and scrub my windows

and water my plants right now,

then I will not have to

do it tomorrow, will I?"

"No," said Frog. "You will not

have to do any of it."

Toad dusted
his chairs.

He scrubbed
his windows.

He watered
his plants.

13

"There,"

said Toad.

"Now I feel better.

I am not

in the dumps anymore."

"Why?" asked Frog.

"Because I have done

all that work," said Toad.

"Now I can save tomorrow

for something that I really want to do."

"What is that?" asked Frog.

14

"Tomorrow," said Toad,

"I can just take life easy."

Toad went back to bed.

He pulled the covers

over his head

and fell asleep.

The Kite

Frog and Toad went out
to fly a kite.
They went to
a large meadow
where the wind was strong.
"Our kite will fly up and up,"
said Frog.
"It will fly all the way up
to the top of the sky."

"Toad," said Frog,

"I will hold the ball of string.

You hold the kite and run."

17

Toad ran across the meadow.

He ran as fast as his short legs
could carry him.

The kite went up in the air.

It fell to the ground with a bump.

Toad heard laughter.

Three robins were sitting in a bush.

"That kite will not fly,"

said the robins.

"You may as well give up."

Toad ran back to Frog.

"Frog," said Toad,

"this kite will not fly.

I give up."

19

"We must make a second try,"
said Frog.

"Wave the kite over your head.
Perhaps that will make it fly."

Toad ran back across the meadow.

He waved the kite over his head.

The kite went up in the air
and then fell down with a thud.
"What a joke!" said the robins.
"That kite will never
get off the ground."

Toad ran back to Frog.

"This kite is a joke," he said.

"It will never get off the ground."

"We have to make

a third try," said Frog.

"Wave the kite over your head

and jump up and down.

Perhaps that will make it fly."

Toad ran across
the meadow again.
He waved the kite
over his head.
He jumped up and down.
The kite went up in the air
and crashed down into the grass.
"That kite is junk,"
said the robins.
"Throw it away and go home."

Toad ran back to Frog.

"This kite is junk," he said.

"I think we should

throw it away and go home."

"Toad," said Frog,

"we need one more try.

Wave the kite over your head.

Jump up and down

and shout UP KITE UP."

Toad ran across the meadow.

He waved the kite over his head.

He jumped up and down.

He shouted, "UP KITE UP!"

The kite flew into the air.

It climbed higher and higher.

"We did it!" cried Toad.

"Yes," said Frog.

"If a running try
did not work,
and a running and waving try
did not work,
and a running, waving,
and jumping try
did not work,
I knew that
a running, waving, jumping,
and shouting try
just had to work."

The robins flew out of the bush.

But they could not fly

as high as the kite.

Frog and Toad sat

and watched their kite.

It seemed to be flying

way up at the top of the sky.

Shivers

The night was cold and dark.

"Listen to the wind
howling in the trees," said Frog.

"What a fine time for a ghost story."

Toad moved deeper into his chair.

"Toad," asked Frog,

"don't you like to be scared?

Don't you like to feel the shivers?"

"I am not too sure," said Toad.

Frog made a fresh pot of tea.

He sat down

and began a story.

29

"When I was small," said Frog,
"my mother and father and I
went out for a picnic.
On the way home we lost our way.
My mother was worried.
'We must get home,' she said.
'We do not want to meet
the Old Dark Frog.'
'Who is that?' I asked.

30

'A terrible ghost,'

said my father.

'He comes out at night and eats

little frog children for supper.' "

Toad sipped his tea.

"Frog," he asked,

"are you making this up?"

"Maybe yes and maybe no,"

said Frog.

"My mother and father
went to search for a path,"
said Frog.
"They told me to wait
until they came back.
I sat under a tree and waited.
The woods became dark.
I was afraid.
Then I saw two huge eyes.
It was the Old Dark Frog.

He was standing near me."

"Frog," asked Toad,

"did this really happen?"

"Maybe it did

and maybe it didn't,"

said Frog.

Frog went on with the story.

"The Dark Frog pulled

a jump rope out of his pocket.

'I am not hungry now,'
said the Dark Frog.
'I have eaten too many
tasty frog children.
But after I jump rope
one hundred times,
I will be hungry again.
Then I will eat YOU!' "

"The Dark Frog tied one end

of the rope to a tree.

'Turn for me!' he shouted.

I turned the rope for the Dark Frog.

He jumped twenty times.

'I am beginning to get hungry,'

said the Dark Frog.

He jumped fifty times.

'I am getting hungrier,'

said the Dark Frog.

He jumped ninety times.

'I am very hungry now!'

said the Dark Frog."

"What happened then?"
asked Toad.

"I had to save my life,"
said Frog.

"I ran around
and around the tree
with the rope.
I tied up
the Old Dark Frog.
He roared and screamed.

I ran away fast."

"I found my mother and father,"
said Frog.

"We came safely home."

"Frog," asked Toad,

"was that a true story?"

"Maybe it was

and maybe it wasn't,"

said Frog.

Frog and Toad sat

close by the fire.

They were scared.

The teacups shook

in their hands.

They were having the shivers.

It was a good, warm feeling.

The Hat

On Toad's birthday

Frog gave him a hat.

Toad was delighted.

"Happy birthday," said Frog.

Toad put on the hat.

It fell down over his eyes.

"I am sorry," said Frog.

"That hat is much too big for you.

I will give you something else."

"No," said Toad. "This hat
is your present to me. I like it.
I will wear it the way it is."

Frog and Toad went for a walk.

Toad tripped over a rock.

He bumped into a tree.

He fell in a hole.

"Frog," said Toad,

"I can't see anything.

I will not be able to wear

your beautiful present.

This is a sad birthday for me."

Frog and Toad
were sad
for a while.
Then Frog said,

"Toad, here is what you must do.

Tonight when you go to bed

you must think

some very big thoughts.

Those big thoughts will make

your head grow larger.

In the morning

your new hat may fit."

"What a good idea," said Toad.

45

That night when Toad went to bed
he thought the biggest thoughts
that he could think.
Toad thought about
giant sunflowers.
He thought about tall oak trees.
He thought about high mountains
covered with snow.

Then Toad fell asleep.

Frog came into Toad's house.

He came in quietly.

Frog found the hat

and took it to his house.

Frog poured some water on the hat.

He put the hat

in a warm place to dry.

It began to shrink.

That hat grew smaller and smaller.

Frog went back to Toad's house.

Toad was still fast asleep.

Frog put the hat back on the hook where he found it.

When Toad woke up in the morning, he put the hat on his head.

It was just the right size.

Toad ran to Frog's house.

"Frog, Frog!" he cried.

"All those big thoughts

have made my head

much larger.

Now I can wear your present!"

Frog and Toad went for a walk.

Toad did not trip

over a rock.

He did not bump into a tree.

He did not fall

in a hole.

It turned out to be

a very pleasant

day after Toad's birthday.

Alone

Toad went to Frog's house.

He found a note on the door.

The note said,

"Dear Toad, I am not at home.

I went out.

I want to be alone."

"Alone?" said Toad.

"Frog has me for a friend.

Why does he want to be alone?"

Toad looked through the windows.

He looked in the garden.

He did not see Frog.

53

Toad went to the woods.

Frog was not there.

He went to the meadow.

Frog was not there.

Toad went down to the river.

There was Frog.

He was sitting on an island

by himself.

"Poor Frog," said Toad.

"He must be very sad.

I will cheer him up."

Toad ran home.

He made sandwiches.

He made a pitcher of iced tea.

He put everything

in a basket.

Toad hurried

back to the river.

"Frog," he shouted,

"it's me.

It's your best friend, Toad!"

Frog was too far away to hear.

Toad took off his jacket

and waved it like a flag.

Frog was too far away to see.

Toad shouted and waved,

but it was no use.

Frog sat on the island.

He did not see or hear Toad.

A turtle swam by.

Toad climbed on the turtle's back.

"Turtle," said Toad,

"carry me to the island.

Frog is there.

He wants to be alone."

"If Frog wants to be alone,"

said the turtle,

"why don't you leave him alone?"

"Maybe you are right," said Toad.

"Maybe Frog does not

want to see me.

Maybe he does not want me

to be his friend anymore."

"Yes, maybe," said the turtle

as he swam to the island.

"Frog!" cried Toad.

"I am sorry for all

the dumb things I do.

I am sorry for all

the silly things I say.

Please be my friend again!"

Toad slipped off the turtle.

With a splash, he fell in the river.

Frog pulled Toad

up onto the island.

Toad looked in the basket.

The sandwiches were wet.

The pitcher of iced tea was empty.

"Our lunch is spoiled," said Toad.

"I made it for you, Frog,

so that you would be happy."

"But Toad," said Frog.

"I *am* happy. I am very happy.

This morning

when I woke up

I felt good because

the sun was shining.

I felt good because

I was a frog.

And I felt good because

I have you for a friend.

I wanted to be alone.

I wanted to think about

how fine everything is."

"Oh," said Toad.
"I guess that is a very good reason
for wanting to be alone."

"Now," said Frog.
"I will be glad *not* to be alone.
Let's eat lunch."

Frog and Toad
stayed on the island
all afternoon.
They ate wet sandwiches
without iced tea.
They were two close friends
sitting alone together.